LITTLE RED RIDING HOOD

A Favorite Story in Rhythm and Rhyme

Retold by JONATHAN PEALE
Illustrations by LUKE SÉGUIN-MAGEE
Music by MARK OBLINGER

CANTATA
LEARNING

WWW.CANTATALEARNING.COM

CANTATA
LEARNING

Published by Cantata Learning
1710 Roe Crest Drive
North Mankato, MN 56003
www.cantatalearning.com

A note to educators and librarians from the publisher: Cantata Learning has provided the following data to assist in book processing and suggested use of Cantata Learning product.

Publisher's Cataloging-in-Publication Data
Prepared by Librarian Consultant: Ann-Marie Begnaud
Library of Congress Control Number: 2016937997
    Little Red Riding Hood : A Favorite Story in Rhythm and Rhyme
    Series: Fairy Tale Tunes
    Retold by Jonathan Peale
    Illustrations by Luke Séguin-Magee
    Music by Mark Oblinger
    Summary: The classic fairy tale of Little Red Riding Hood retold in song, with full-color illustrations.
    ISBN: 978-1-63290-769-1 (library binding/CD)
Suggested Dewey and Subject Headings:
    Dewey: E 398.2
    LCSH Subject Headings: Fairy tales – Juvenile literature. | Fairy tales – Songs and music – Texts. | Fairy tales – Juvenile sound recordings.
    Sears Subject Headings: Fairy tales. | Folklore. | School songbooks. | Children's songs.
    BISAC Subject Headings: JUVENILE FICTION / Fairy Tales & Folklore / Adaptations. | JUVENILE FICTION / Stories in Verse. | JUVENILE FICTION / Animals / Wolves & Coyotes.

Book design and art direction: Tim Palin Creative
Editorial direction: Flat Sole Studio
Music direction: Elizabeth Draper
Music written and produced by Mark Oblinger

Printed in the United States of America in North Mankato, Minnesota.
122016   0339CGS17

ACCESS THE MUSIC!

SCAN CODE WITH MOBILE APP

CANTATALEARNING.COM

TIPS TO SUPPORT LITERACY AT HOME

WHY READING AND SINGING WITH YOUR CHILD IS SO IMPORTANT

Daily reading with your child leads to increased academic achievement. Music and songs, specifically rhyming songs, are a fun and easy way to build early literacy and language development. Music skills correlate significantly with both phonological awareness and reading development. Singing helps build vocabulary and speech development. And reading and appreciating music together is a wonderful way to strengthen your relationship.

READ AND SING EVERY DAY!

TIPS FOR USING CANTATA LEARNING BOOKS AND SONGS DURING YOUR DAILY STORY TIME

1. As you sing and read, point out the different words on the page that rhyme. Suggest other words that rhyme.

2. Memorize simple rhymes such as Itsy Bitsy Spider and sing them together. This encourages comprehension skills and early literacy skills.

3. Use the questions in the back of each book to guide your singing and storytelling.

4. Read the included sheet music with your child while you listen to the song. How do the music notes correlate to the words of the song?

5. Sing along on the go and at home. Access music by scanning the QR code on each Cantata book, or by using the included CD. You can also stream or download the music for free to your computer, smartphone, or mobile device.

Devoting time to daily reading shows that you are available for your child. Together, you are building language, literacy, and listening skills.

Have fun reading and singing!

The story of a little girl in a red hooded cape walking to her grandmother's house has been told for hundreds of years. Like many fairy tales, this story has a **moral**. It teaches children to **obey** their parents and not talk to strangers.

To find out if Red Riding Hood gets away from the Big Bad Wolf, turn the page and sing along!

"Your grandmother's sick and lying in bed,"
Little Red Riding Hood's mother said.
"I've packed her a basket of apples and bread."

Get on your way, Red Riding Hood!

Little Red left with her basket and all.

She walked through the woods
where the brown leaves fall.

She met a big wolf that was hairy and tall.

Get on your way, Red Riding Hood!

"Where are you going?" the Wolf **slyly** said.

"To visit my grandmother lying in bed.

I really can't stop to talk," replied Red.

Get on your way, Red Riding Hood!

Red hurried away, but the Wolf quickly sped.

He reached Granny's house first and found her in bed.

He **swallowed** her down and then sweetly said,

"Come inside, Red Riding Hood!"

9

Isn't she brave?

Isn't she good?

She wears her red hood

when she walks through the wood.

Be careful!

Be careful, Little Red Riding Hood!

Red Riding Hood knocked,
   and the Wolf said, "Come in."
He held the blankets up close to his chin.
"Come close to your Granny," he said with a grin.

Run away, Red Riding Hood!

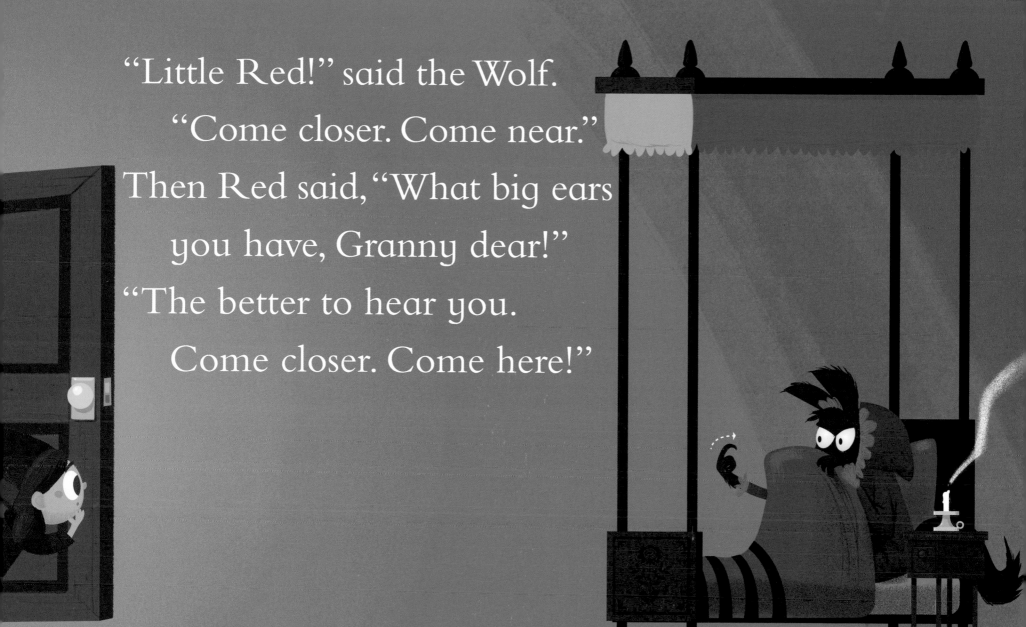

"Little Red!" said the Wolf.
"Come closer. Come near."
Then Red said, "What big ears
you have, Granny dear!"
"The better to hear you.
Come closer. Come here!"

Run away, Red Riding Hood!

Isn't she brave?
Isn't she good?

She wears her red hood
when she walks through the wood.

Be careful!

Be careful, Little Red Riding Hood!

"What big eyes you have, oh, Grandmother dear."
"The better to see you. It's so dark in here,"
the Wolf said. "Come to your Granny. Come near!"

He will eat you, Red Riding Hood!

"What big eyes you have,
   oh, Grandmother dear!"
"The better to see you.
   It's so dark in here."
"What big teeth you have!
   They fill me with fear!"

"The better to eat you, Red Riding Hood!"

Red Riding Hood gasped.

"Someone help me!" she cried.

A big, strong **lumberjack** who was walking outside rushed into the house with his **axe** sharp and wide.

That mean wolf is dead, Red Riding Hood!

Then Granny popped out.
She hugged little Red.
They smiled at the lumberjack.
"Thank you!" they said.
Then Granny said, "Rats!
There's wolf hair in my bed!"

That mean wolf is dead, Red Riding Hood!

Isn't she brave?
Isn't she good?

She wears her red hood
when she walks through the wood.

Be careful!

Be careful, Little Red Riding Hood!

SONG LYRICS
Little Red Riding Hood

"Your grandmother's sick and lying in bed,"
Little Red Riding Hood's mother said.
"I've packed her a basket of apples and bread."

    Get on your way, Red Riding Hood!

Little Red left with her basket and all.
She walked through the woods where the
    brown leaves fall.
She met a big wolf that was hairy and tall.

    Get on your way, Red Riding Hood!

"Where are you going?" the Wolf slyly said.
"To visit my grandmother lying in bed.
I really can't stop to talk," replied Red.

    Get on your way, Red Riding Hood!

Red hurried away, but the Wolf quickly sped.
He reached Granny's house first and found
    her in bed.
He swallowed her down and then sweetly said,
    "Come inside, Red Riding Hood!"

Isn't she brave?
Isn't she good?
She wears her red hood
when she walks through the wood.
Be careful!
Be careful, Little Red Riding Hood!

Red Riding Hood knocked, and the Wolf
    said, "Come in."
He held the blankets up close to his chin.
"Come close to your Granny," he said with
    a grin.

    Run away, Red Riding Hood!

"Little Red!" said the Wolf. "Come closer.
    Come near."
Then Red said, "What big ears you have,
    Granny dear!"
"The better to hear you. Come closer.
    Come here!"

    Run away, Red Riding Hood!

Isn't she brave?
Isn't she good?
She wears her red hood
when she walks through the wood.
Be careful!
Be careful, Little Red Riding Hood!

"What big eyes you have, oh,
    Grandmother dear."
"The better to see you. It's so dark in here,"
the Wolf said. "Come to your Granny.
    Come near!"

    He will eat you, Red Riding Hood!

"What big eyes you have, oh,
    Grandmother dear!"
"The better to see you. It's so dark in here."
"What big teeth you have! They fill me
    with fear!"

    "The better to eat you, Red Riding Hood!"

Red Riding Hood gasped. "Someone help
    me!" she cried.
A strong lumberjack who was walking outside
rushed into the house with his axe sharp
    and wide.

    That mean wolf is dead, Red Riding Hood!

Then Granny popped out. She hugged
    little Red.
They smiled at the lumberjack. "Thank you!"
    they said.
Then Granny said, "Rats! There's wolf hair in
    my bed!"

    That mean wolf is dead, Red Riding Hood!

Isn't she brave?
Isn't she good?
She wears her red hood
when she walks through the wood.
Be careful!
Be careful, Little Red Riding Hood!

Little Red Riding Hood

Musical Theater
Mark Oblinger

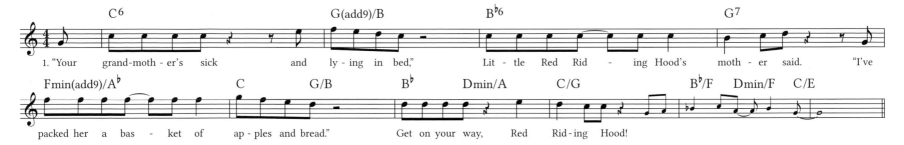

1. "Your grand-moth-er's sick and ly-ing in bed," Lit-tle Red Rid-ing Hood's moth-er said. "I've packed her a bas-ket of ap-ples and bread." Get on your way, Red Rid-ing Hood!

Verse 2
Little Red left with her basket and all.
She walked through the woods where the brown leaves fall.
She met a big wolf that was hairy and tall.

Get on your way, Red Riding Hood!

Verse 3
"Where are you going?" the Wolf slyly said.
"To visit my grandmother lying in bed.
I really can't stop to talk," replied Red.

Get on your way, Red Riding Hood!

Verse 4
Red hurried away, but the Wolf quickly sped.
He reached Granny's house first and found her in bed.
He swallowed her down and then sweetly said,

"Come inside, Red Riding Hood!"

Chorus

Is-n't she brave? Is-n't she good? She wears her red hood when she walks through the wood. Be care-ful! Be care-ful, Lit-tle Red Rid-ing Hood!

Verse 5
Red Riding Hood knocked, and the Wolf said, "Come in."
He held the blankets up close to his chin.
"Come close to your Granny," he said with a grin.

Run away, Red Riding Hood!

Verse 6
"Little Red!" said the Wolf. "Come closer. Come near."
Then Red said, "What big ears you have, Granny dear!"
"The better to hear you. Come closer. Come here!"

Run away, Red Riding Hood!

Chorus

Verse 7
"What big eyes you have, oh, Grandmother dear."
"The better to see you. It's so dark in here,"
the Wolf said. "Come to your Granny. Come near!"

He will eat you, Red Riding Hood!

Verse 8
"What big eyes you have, oh, Grandmother dear!"
"The better to see you. It's so dark in here."
"What big teeth you have! They fill me with fear!"

"The better to eat you, Red Riding Hood!"

Verse 9
Red Riding Hood gasped. "Someone help me!" she cried.
A strong lumberjack who was walking outside
rushed into the house with his axe sharp and wide.

That mean wolf is dead, Red Riding Hood!

Verse 10
Then Granny popped out. She hugged little Red.
They smiled at the lumberjack. "Thank you!" they said.
Then Granny said, "Rats! There's wolf hair in my bed!"

That mean wolf is dead, Red Riding Hood!

Chorus

GLOSSARY

axe—a tool with a sharp blade used to chop wood

lumberjack—a worker who cuts down trees

moral—a lesson to be learned from a story

obey—to do what someone tells you to do

slyly—to do something in a secretive and sneaky way

GUIDED READING ACTIVITIES

1. Red Riding Hood walks through the woods to her grandmother's house. On the way, she meets the Big Bad Wolf. Draw another animal that she might meet.

2. Red Riding Hood makes both good and bad choices in this story. What is the best choice she makes? What is the worst?

3. Red Riding Hood helps her grandmother by bringing her snacks. How do you help other people?

TO LEARN MORE

Frampton, Otis. *Red Riding Hood, Superhero*. North Mankato, MN: Capstone, 2015.

Gunderson, Jessica. *Little Red Riding Hood: Three Beloved Tales*. North Mankato, MN: Capstone, 2015.

Smith, Alex. *Little Red and the Very Hungry Lion*. New York: Scholastic, 2016.

Woolvin, Bethan. *Little Red*. Atlanta: Peachtree Publishers, 2016.